CHILDREN'S STORIES

Volume 6

Tales of the Wild West Series

Rick Steber

Illustrations by Don Gray

NOTE

CHILDREN'S STORIES is the sixth book in the Tales of the Wild West Series

CHILDREN'S STORIES
Volume 6
Tales of the Wild West Series

ISBN 0-945134-06-1

Bonanza Publishing
Box 204
Prineville, Oregon 97754

Tales of the Wild West

INTRODUCTION

The first white children to come west were sons and daughters of the pioneers. They rode horseback or trudged barefooted beside the wagons across the Great Plains and over the mountains. Some fell victim to disease or accidents and were buried beside the Oregon Trail.

Those who survived found a wonderful playground out west. There were wide-open spaces, slow-moving streams and deep, dark forests. Mothers watched over their young because if a child wandered away, he or she might be carried off by wild animals.

Children of the frontier were seasoned to a hard life. They had to be strong and resilient and were forced to grow up quickly. By the time a boy was eight or nine he knew how to handle a rifle and hunt wild game for meat. He helped his father clearing land, splitting rails, building fence and farming with a team of horses. Girls worked beside their mothers; picking wild berries, making lye soap, rendering hogs, washing on a scrub board and cooking over a woodstove. The list of time-consuming chores seemed endless. By the time a girl was fourteen or fifteen she was ready to marry and start a family of her own.

NARROW ESCAPE

Elizabeth Sager, who was six years old when her family started over the Oregon Trail in 1844, recalled a harrowing incident that happened along the way. "I couldn't rightly say where we were at the time except to tell you it was in sagebrush country and as dry as dry could be. One morning a friend of mine, Alvira Edes, suggested we take a walk to get ahead of the wagon train and out of the dust. We were hoping to find water.

"We had hiked maybe a mile and, finding no water and no prospects of water, Alvira suggested we turn up a little draw. She said, 'See those trees? I bet there is a spring there. We can have a drink and catch the wagons before they cross over the hill.'

"Off we went, but upon reaching the cluster of trees, much to our disappointment, there was no water. We kept climbing, were soon lost and walked for hours in the heat of the burning sun. I was afraid we might be left to wander aimlessly until we died. It was a terrible, terrible feeling to be lost like that.

"We stumbled on and finally, topping a little rise, way off in the distance could be seen canvas covers. A more beautiful sight my eyes have never witnessed! We forgot our fatigue and ran forward until at last we came to the wagons. I called to my brother, who was driving the team, to help me up but he told me, 'You'll have to wait until we get to the top of the hill.'

"That was too much for me. I sank down in the sand beside the road and began to cry. Brother relented, lifted me into the wagon and we continued on. Never again did I wander far from the wagons."

SPYGLASS

"Father was an early day pioneer in the Puget Sound area. Mother was Indian. They met, fell in love, got married and for a number of years operated a trading post on Whidbey Island," told Louisa Sinclair.

"My first recollections as a child are of living on the island — playing along the beach, picking up bright pebbles and being entertained by Indians and a few white men at the trading post. There were very few children and I admit I was a bit pampered and spoiled by the adults.

"Mother taught me how to sew and, using patterns and material from the store, I made shirts for the men and they paid me handsomely for my efforts. Too, I liked to pick up shells and colored pebbles and I made these into knick-knacks and picture frames by embedding the bright-colored shells and pebbles in putty. These I sold for a good price. I always had money.

"One afternoon several men were sitting on the porch in front of the trading post watching the approach of a sailing ship. They were wagering as to which of the several vessels plying the Sound this might be. The ship was too far away to be recognized, so I went inside the trading post, got Father's spyglass and saw the ship's name. I rejoined the men on the porch and very innocently commented, 'May I be allowed to bet?'

"They laughed and told me to specify the amount I wished to wager and the name of the ship. I told them, 'I will bet $5 that it is the *Walter Ellis*,' and, of course, when the ship came in they had to pay me."

COPPER PENNY

One winter day in 1910 three-year-old Lawrence Johnson was playing on the floor. He found a penny, picked it up, looked at it and then popped it in his mouth.

"Lawrence, do you have something in your mouth?" his mother asked as she entered the room. Lawrence shook his head no, and swallowed. The copper penny lodged in his esophagus. He coughed a time or two and his mother turned him over her knee and patted him on his back, but he could not dislodge the penny. Mrs. Johnson held Lawrence on her lap and demanded to know, "What did you have in your mouth?"

He lied and told her, "Nothing."

Several days passed and Lawrence seemed to be having trouble swallowing. He was losing weight. And he had been rubbing at his throat so much that the skin was red and irritated. Mrs. Johnson took Lawrence to a doctor. He poked and probed at the boy's throat before finally turning to Mrs. Johnson and asking, "Could he have swallowed something? Perhaps a coin?"

"The other day I thought he had something in his mouth but he swallowed it before I could see what it was. He coughed once or twice but he never gagged or anything. I suppose he could have found a coin on the floor," said Mrs. Johnson.

"This could be very serious," the doctor said. "I propose an operation. If we do not remove it, gangrene may set in and your son could die."

Two surgeons removed the penny from Lawrence's throat. The operation was an unqualified success and was heralded, at the time, as one of the most unique operations in the history of medicine.

STEALING A STAR

The Hughes family lived a quiet life on their rural farm in the Willamette Valley of Oregon, until the afternoon in 1902 when Ellis happened across an unusual, bell-shaped rock with holes in it like Swiss cheese. He rushed home and told his wife and fifteen-year-old son Ed, "I think I've found a fallen star."

The problem with the discovery was that the meteorite was on neighboring property belonging to the Oregon Iron and Steel Company. Ellis and Ed immediately started clearing a path from their property to the meteorite. Upon reaching it they jacked the 15½-ton rock onto a stout cart and used a horse-drawn windlass to winch the rock to their backyard.

Word of the discovery spread like wildfire and the curious who came for a look were charged a quarter. One of the sightseers was an attorney for the Oregon Iron and Steel Company. The company brought suit. In court Ellis contended the meteorite was actually an abandoned Indian relic and free for the taking. He called two Clackamas Indians to the witness stand and they testified their tribe once worshipped the stone and before battle the braves dipped their arrows in the water that collected in the holes. This brought a chorus of laughter in the courtroom. The verdict went in favor of the company. Ellis appealed to the Oregon Supreme Court but he lost once again.

The Oregon Iron and Steel Company took possession of the meteorite and sold it for $26,000 to New York socialite, Mrs. William Dodge, II. She donated it to New York's Hayden Planetarium where the treasure remains on display. The plaque beneath it reads, "Willamette Meteorite — The largest meteorite ever found in the United States." But it does not tell anything of the work and heartbreak of the man and boy 3,000 miles away who discovered it and brought it to the attention of the world.

WINDY

Wind and rain lashed the Pacific coast as a mare gave birth to a beautiful black filly with a perfect white star on her forehead.

By morning the storm had passed and the sun was breaking through. A small band of horses walked the beach and the newborn filly was with them. She paused to smell a chunk of foam brought in by the storm and, on spindly legs, she galloped to catch up to the other horses.

During the day the little band wandered through the shifting dunes or along the shore where waves hard-packed the sand. When they were hungry or thirsty they traveled to the estuaries and fed on lush grass and drank from the mirrored surface of fresh water lakes. At night the mustangs traveled inland and sought protection in thickets of stunted pine.

One hot summer day a group of mounted cowboys surprised the band of mustangs and managed to rope the leader and all the other horses, except for the black filly with the perfect white star. She broke free and ran away.

Cowboy Ted Dooley recalled, "We tried to get a rope on that filly but she was just too fast. She could run like the wind. Me and some of the boys, we named her Windy."

As the horses were herded away Windy stood on top of a sand dune and watched. Windy was alone and in the days and nights to come she avoided all contact with humans. But occasionally, on a moonlit night, a beachcomber would report seeing a horse, mane and tail flowing in the wind, running along a lonely stretch of beach.

Over the years many cowboys tried to capture the elusive black mustang. But Windy knew the coils of rope they carried would choke off her freedom and she would race away like a dancing whirlwind. For all of her 34 years of life Windy ran free and wild.

OUR TRIP WEST

"I was a young lad of 13 when our family came west over the Oregon Trail," recalled Al Hawk. "We made it across the plains and over the Rocky Mountains. Along the Snake River we were met by two white men who convinced Father the Snake River could be run all the way to the Columbia River, and they claimed from there it was an easy float to the Willamette Valley. They talked Father into selling them our loose stock.

"We fashioned a raft and used the wagon bed to hold all of our possessions. But Father must not have been entirely convinced the river could be run because he employed Mr. Cline to drive our team and the running gear of our wagon along the trail.

"We put in below Salmon Falls and for a while we drifted along at a pleasant four miles per hour. But we soon found ourselves trapped in a strong current that pulled us into a rapid. We were at the mercy of the angry water. And there was not a single rapid but a series of rapids. We managed to paddle ashore where the women and children debarked and portaged around.

"After ten days engaged in the struggle of guiding the raft through the dangerous water our hearts were made glad by the surprise appearance of Mr. Cline. Short work was made of hoisting the water-soaked wagon bed back onto the running gear. Once again we rolled across the prairie.

"It was in that manner that we struggled west. Finally, after nine months and ten days on the trail, we reached the Willamette Valley of Oregon."

OREGON TRAIL MEMORIES

"The spring of 1846 Father, Mother and nine of us children started over the Oregon Trail," recalled Mary Munkers. "There were about 50 wagons in our wagon train when we pulled out of St. Joe, Missouri.

"I was ten years old, interested in everything and as I could see better afoot than in the dusty wagon, I walked. One of my jobs was to gather buffalo chips as we traveled. When we stopped Mother used them to make a fire. At first it was hard on her and the other women to cook without wood but they soon became expert at building a fire using buffalo chips.

"One of my most vivid recollections of our trip west is of the night a frightening storm descended upon us when we were camped out on the Plains. The wind came up and blew something frightful, flattening our tents and ripping loose the canvas covers from the wagons. One moment the night would be black as ink and the next brilliant flashes of lightning would light up our surroundings as bright as day. Thunder boomed and crashed around us. And then it began to rain and it seemed as if the sky were a huge lake that was constantly slopping over and drenching us to the bone. We were wet, cold and paralyzed with fear.

"The men spent the best part of the night trying to keep the oxen and cattle from stampeding but they stampeded in spite of their efforts. We had to lay over the next day to round up the stock and to get things fixed as best we could. But we were soon traveling once again, continuing on our way west."

STORY OF MY LIFE

"Father was a French-Canadian and came into the Northwest in the early days before the country was settled. For a time he was in the employ of the Hudson's Bay Fur Company but when he married Mother — she was French-Canadian and Indian — he quit the Company and they took a land claim along the Columbia River. Father built a fine, two-story, hand-hewn log house with two fireplaces. He made all the furniture himself. I was born there in the home place in 1852,"related Louise Jondrau.

"There were twelve children in our family, six boys and six girls. I worked very hard when I was a child, helping with the housework as well as in the fields. One of my jobs was to cut tule reeds. They were like cattails and grew in abundance around our place. Mother and my sisters and I wove the tule reeds into mats that we sold to the settlers.

"In those days our neighbors would often get together for dances and picnics, along with an occasional horse race. During the Christmas season we had very good feeds; wild game, baked salmon, chicken, roast pig. There was not much drinking, just a little liquor for the men. Mother employed an Indian woman to stay in our cabin with the young children while the rest of us went to the feast and we would dance all night, go home to sleep and be back the next night to party again. We had such lovely times.

"I speak English, French and Chinook but never went to school a day in my life. There were no schools around those parts. I married at the age of 15 years, early marriages were the custom, and I wore a calico dress and moccasins on my wedding day. I have seven children, ten grandchildren and two great-grandchildren.

"That is pretty much the story of my life — kids and a lot of hard work."

MULESKINNER

Some of the most important men of the Old West were the muleskinners. They delivered mail, food and supplies to scattered settlements and remote mining camps. Their teams of mules crossed dry deserts and climbed mountain passes on trails that were narrow and steep.

The ultimate freighting outfit consisted of eight or ten mules working as a team to pull two heavily-loaded wagons, one hitched behind the other. Mules were prized for their size, pulling power and stamina. A good mule could cost several hundred dollars, on up to a thousand dollars or more.

Because of the sizeable investment a skinner always took good care of his mules. On steep grades the animals were rested frequently and a driver never started a pull if even one of his animals was still breathing hard. After a day's work all the mules were rubbed down, curry combed, watered and fed hay and grain.

Mules were driven with lines and a series of voice commands. If a mule became complacent, or did not follow commands, the muleskinner was likely to let loose with a verbal barrage. A polite term for this normally coarse language was "mule talk". And usually the mule talk was punctuated with the popping of a bullwhip.

Completing the first-class muleskinner's outfit were bells on the hames. The bells served two purposes. On narrow trails they allowed other teamsters to time their passing for a wide spot in the road. They also identified a particular muleskinner long before he came into view. People waiting for a part, a tool, or expecting something special would be alerted and come to meet the teamster.

BANISHED

Newt Thomas was a young boy the summer of 1851 when his family emigrated west over the Oregon Trail. In later years he enjoyed reminiscing about the experience.

"There was a friend of mine, Steve, who was a few years older than me. He was traveling alone, driving a wagon for his board. And there was a girl on the train, a very pretty young girl with long, curly blonde hair.

"There came a day when a band of Indians rode into camp and one of the braves made sign he wanted to trade for the girl. Even though he was rebuked he persisted. Finally, thinking he was making a joke, Steve said, 'All right, you can have her for six ponies.'

"The next morning the Indian drove six horses into our camp and insisted on taking the girl. The men of the wagon train ran the Indian out of camp but they were so mad at Steve for putting all of us in a dangerous situation they held a meeting and decided to banish poor Steve.

"All us kids liked Steve. We saved food from our meals and when we broke camp we would leave it in a conspicuous place. Years later I was running a pack string of mules to the mines in the Boise Basin of Idaho. One evening I came to a remote cabin and stopped to ask if I could put up there for the night. Much to my surprise the fellow living there called me by name. When I questioned how he knew my name he informed me he was Steve. He went on to tell me that he had eaten the food we left for him and that he had hidden from the Indians during the day and had traveled at night. He eventually came upon a wagon train that had laid over on account all the people were sick with dysentery. He nursed them back to health and in return they brought him through."

THE CURE

Sixteen-year-old Charlie Seeber was sick with tuberculosis. The doctor told his parents, "If I were you I would move somewhere with a dry climate. The higher the altitude the better. If you stay here Charlie will die."

The Seebers moved to Enterprise, Oregon and Charlie began hiking into the Wallowa Mountains. Weeks passed and the fresh mountain air and exercise seemed to revive Charlie and to heal his tuberculosis. His wheezing and fits of coughing became less intense.

Perhaps because of his illness Charlie's hair turned prematurely white. He was given the nickname "Silver Tip". Hikers in the mountains reported seeing him and they always commented on his white hair, his piercing blue, half-wild eyes and the calm demeanor of the lean young man.

Charlie built a number of log cabins in the back country and moved from cabin to cabin as the mood struck him. For the most part he lived off the land, taking what Mother Nature provided. When sheep were introduced into the area in the early 1900s Charlie fought the Forest Service and the sheepmen. Sometimes he took potshots at the sheep to scare them away and prevent overgrazing of a fragile high-mountain meadow.

Charlie lived in the Wallowa Mountains for many, many years. The frail young boy, who doctors said would never live to see his 17th birthday, lived to be 102 years old.

DAREDEVIL OF THE SKY

Silas Christofferson introduced the West to aviation. He was a daredevil of the sky.

He established a world distance record, flying 302 miles between San Francisco and Los Angeles, and the world altitude record with a 14,500-foot flight over Mt. Whitney. But Silas is best known for his death-defying stunt — attempting to fly off the roof of the Multnomah Hotel during the 1912 Portland Rose Festival.

Asked why he was willing to attempt such a feat, Silas replied, "I will be the first in the history of aviation. It was only nine years ago that the Wright brothers first flew. I am not unaware of the danger but I have every confidence in myself."

The airplane, patterned after the Curtiss Pusher with an engine and propeller mounted behind the pilot, was dismantled and hauled up the outside of the hotel with ropes. It was reassembled at one end of a platform built on the roof.

June 11, 1912 dawned gray and drizzly. A crowd of 50,000 spectators jammed downtown streets. Some leaned precariously from windows or hung from fire escapes, craning their necks to catch a glimpse as Silas settled himself at the controls of his airplane. He nodded his head, the propeller was spun and the motor roared to life.

Silas released the brake and the flimsy kite-like craft shot down the runway. The plane was at the edge of the roof, where either a flight or a fatality had to occur. The crowd gave a collective gasp and then wildly cheered for the daredevil.

Silas disappeared into the clouds. He flew over the Columbia River and twelve minutes later he touched down on the polo grounds at the Vancouver Army barracks.

ICE HARVEST

In the old days, before there were refrigerators, it was common practice to cut pond ice in the winter and store it for use during the months of warm weather.

The harvesting of ice normally began in December when the ice was 12 to 14 inches thick. Each worker on the crew had a certain task. The groover walked behind a horse-drawn plow fitted with chisels spaced about 30 inches apart. The cutter, wielding a long metal saw with two-inch teeth, cut the ice into blocks. Pushers used long-handled pike poles to float the blocks to a chute where men hooked iron tongs on the blocks and pulled them up a chute and into the back of a sled.

Horses pulled the loaded wagon to a well-insulated ice storage shed. The floor was covered with a layer of sawdust for additional insulation. The ice was unloaded down an incline and skillfully stacked by pilers so the blocks fit together tightly. Small chunks of ice and shavings were used to fill any air space and a small quantity of water was poured over each layer to insure the joints would freeze together. The object was to make the entire mass a solid block of ice. More sawdust was piled over and around this ice block.

During warm weather months, the iceman loaded his wagon with ice in the early morning and distributed blocks to customers around town. Even on the hottest days of summer there was ice for lemonade.

THE NEWSPAPER

Nearly a hundred years ago a teacher gave her pupils the assignment of writing an essay on the definition of a newspaper. A twelve-year-old boy wrote the following:

"Newspapers are sheets of paper on which stuff to read is printed. The men look over the paper to see if their name is printed in it and the women use it to put on their shelves and such. I don't know how newspapers came into the world. I don't think God does, either. The Bible says nothing about editors and I have never heard about one being in heaven. I guess the editor is the missing link them fellars talk about.

"The first editor I ever heard of was the one that wrote up the flood. He has been here in town ever since.

"Some editors belong to the church and some try to raise whiskers. All of them raise hell in their neighborhoods and all of them are liars, at least all I know and I only know one.

"Editors never die. At least I never saw a dead one. Sometimes the paper dies and then people feel glad but someone starts it up again.

"Our paper is a poor one but we take it so Ma can put it on the pantry shelves. Our editor don't amount to much but Pa says he had a poor chance when he was a boy. He goes without underclothes in the winter, wears no socks, and has a wife to support him.

"Pa hasn't paid his subscription in five years and don't intend to."

STRANGE WHITE WOMAN

Catherine Haun was a young bride when she and her husband started west following the gold rush of 1849. Near Fort Laramie members of the wagon train celebrated Independence Day with a dance held under the stars.

"During the celebration a strange white woman, with a little girl in her sheltering embrace, rushed up to the dancers," Catherine recalled. "She was trembling with terror, tottering with hunger, her hair was disheveled and her clothing was badly torn. The child crouched with fear in the folds of her mother's tattered skirt.

"This woman could give no account of her forlorn condition, except to sob, 'Indians'. But after she had partaken of food and was refreshed by a safe night's rest she told us that her husband and sister had contracted cholera and died and that their wagon had been forced to drop from the wagon train they had been traveling with. Indians attacked and her son and her brother were killed. She was obliged to flee for her life, dragging her 5-year-old daughter.

"In order to avoid Indians she concealed herself and her daughter in the trees and boulders much of the time. They ate a raw fish she caught with her hands and a squirrel she killed with a stone. That was all they had had to eat in 3 days. Our music and the smell of cooking food had attracted her to our camp.

"Martha, for that was her name, pleaded with us to return her and her child to her home state of Wisconsin. But we had gone too far on the road and there was no alternative for her but to accept our protection and continue on with us to California."

FISHING TRIP

One beautiful day in the fall of 1893 Willie Turner and Jack Caviness kissed their mothers good-by and rode out of town toward a secret mountain lake to spend an entire week camping and fishing.

Willie and Jack rode horseback into the foothills and their dogs trailed along. After a long, steep climb they topped out on a ridge overlooking a sparkling blue lake tucked into the folds of a timbered valley. They galloped off the hill and raced to see who would be the first to cut a willow pole and get his line in the water.

Before they got around to setting camp they had a heavy stringer of fish, more than enough for dinner. Their luck held for the next several days. They ate fish at every meal. In fact, they were getting tired of the steady diet and when a deer wandered near camp they shot it and feasted on venison steaks.

That night they were awakened by the dogs and it was evident from the way they were barking, growling and snarling that a wild animal was trying to reach the meat hanging in a tree.

In the pale light of a new day the boys found the carcass of the deer missing and tracks of a huge mountain lion in the soft dirt. They saddled the horses, grabbed their rifles and turned the dogs loose.

The dogs took off through the timber and in less than a minute were barking excitedly on a hot trail. The big cat, with his belly full of meat, ran a short distance and treed. He lay stretched on a high limb, hissing and taking swipes at the dogs as they bayed and leaped in the air.

Willie and Jack reached the scene and fired their rifles simultaneously. The mountain lion tumbled out of the tree. He was one of the biggest cats ever killed. From the tip of his nose to the tip of his tail he measured 10 feet 7 inches.

THE TERRIBLE FALL

Twice a day, on the way to and from school, the Graber, Filson and Blake children had to cross a frightfully high railroad bridge. Before venturing onto the quarter-mile trestle the children always stopped and listened, making sure no trains were approaching. Then, two-by-two and holding hands, stepping from one tie to the next, they hurried across. They were very cautious.

One day in the spring of 1904 the children were crossing the trestle on their way home from school when a gust of wind blew little Lena Graber's hat off her head. Without thinking she let go of the other girl's hand, reached for the hat and fell off the trestle without making a sound.

The girls screamed, turned around and ran back to the school to tell their teacher. The boys, Marion Filson and Charlie Blake, scrambled down the rocky wall of the ravine, hollering as they went, "Lena! Lena! Are you all right?"

Not for several terrifying minutes did Lena respond and then, in a weak voice, she called, "Here I am."

The boys found Lena clutching a small pine tree. "I'm all right," she informed them.

Charlie told her, "Walk." And she walked.

Marion said, "Can you move your arms?" She moved her arms.

Lena suffered no broken bones. She did not have any cuts, contusions or bruises. She had not even torn her clothing. Evidently the supple pine tree had broken her 85-foot fall and saved her life. But the consequences of what might have happened were clearly visible. The lunch basket she had been carrying had been smashed into pieces on the rocks.

LOOP-DE-LOOP

John Larsen was a professional entertainer who traveled the West staging death-defying exhibitions. His biggest show of all was at the 1902 Portland, Oregon Elks carnival where he promised to risk his life attempting a full loop-de-loop on a bicycle.

John, dressed in red, was poised at the top of a treacherous incline. Bugles sounded. Drums rolled. A spotlight danced gaily over the scene. At last John pushed off and pedaled his bicycle furiously down the steep incline leading to the loop-de-loop. Faster! Faster! John could not control the bike. The front wheel came off the track but a net above the crowd fortunately caught John and his bicycle.

John remounted the scaffolding. But his second attempt was also a failure. A murmur ran through the crowd and the general feeling was that the loop-de-loop was an impossible feat. But John raised his hands to silence the doubters and he vowed, "Ladies and Gentlemen. I promise I will complete the loop-de-loop."

On the third try the daredevil hit the loop-de-loop in perfect fashion. The bike flew through the heart of the loop, and then, on the backside, the front wheel collapsed under the force of the tight turn and, once again, the bicycle and rider were tossed into the protective netting. This time the crowd stood and cheered loudly because the loop-de-loop had finally been conquered.

THE WONDER DOG

Bobbie was a bob-tailed Scotch collie and shepherd mix, a fine-looking dog with long hair and floppy ears. He belonged to Frank and Elizabeth Brazier of Silverton, Oregon and their daughters Nova and Leona. In August 1923 the Braziers embarked on a cross-country trip in an Overland Red Bird automobile. Bobbie rode outside on the top of the luggage rack.

The ninth day of the trip they stopped for gas in Wolcott, Indiana. Frank was inside paying when he heard Bobbie bark. He rushed outside and saw several dogs chasing Bobbie around a corner. The Braziers spent the next several days looking but could not find Bobbie. Though they hated to leave, they had to continue on.

According to the story pieced together later, Bobbie spent several weeks wandering blindly before getting his bearings and turning west. Men in a hobo camp recalled sharing mulligan stew with him, he stayed with a sheepherder and a rancher, but for the most part Bobbie dodged humans.

Six months to the day after Bobbie was lost Nova and a girlfriend were walking down the main street of Silverton. All of a sudden Nova seized her girlfriend by the arm and exclaimed, "Isn't that Bobbie?" She called, "Bobbie!" and the dog, emaciated and limping in pain, came to her and licked her face.

Practically every newspaper in the United States ran a story about Bobbie's amazing 3,000-mile journey home. Robert Ripley's *Believe It or Not* radio show featured Bobbie, a book was written, and Bobbie even starred in his own movie, *Bobbie, The Wonder Dog.*

Gray

GRANDMA

Grandma McAllister rocked back and forth in her old rocking chair and remembered. "Father was the first white man to set foot in the Nisqually Valley. That was even before Washington was a territory.

"He built us a fine house but it was up to Mother and my sisters and me to decorate it and make it a home. We covered the walls with brown Indian mats, put a tanned ox hide on the floor for a rug, and even sewed curtains with a little fringe to pretty them up. Mother took precious window glass and made some mirrors by tacking pieces of a worn out black shawl behind the glass. She made one for each of us girls.

"At Christmas Father would tan a hide and pay a neighbor, who had a background as a cobbler, to make us kids shoes. Although they were not handsome the shoes were extremely durable.

"It was always big news when we heard another group of emigrants was coming our way. We picked vegetables from our garden and met the travelers along the road. Oftentimes the appreciative pioneers would try to pay Mother but she declined, saying, 'You will do me a favor by keeping the money and instead allow me to trace any clothes patterns you may have.'

"By doing that my sisters and I always had something new to sew and if not in the latest style our clothes were close to the latest style. That's just the way it was back in the pioneering days. You made do with what you could get hold of."

BRUNO

The summer of 1934 Tom and Joe Perez went on a camping trip to the mountains. When the brothers returned home they had a black bear cub with them.

"What in the heck are you going to do with that cub?" their father wanted to know.

"Teach him tricks and train him to wrestle," Tom said. "Then we're gonna travel the countryside putting on shows. We'll make a fortune."

The brothers named the cub Bruno. They built a cage in the backyard and began the training process. The following summer they purchased a touring automobile, painted it a rainbow of bright colors, and chained Bruno in the back seat. All they had to do was drive from one town to the next, make a couple sashays up and down the main street, and a full house at that evening's show was all but ensured.

Each well-rehearsed performance began with Bruno dancing in an adorable skirt. Then the bear rolled a barrel on the ground, did a few somersaults and jumped through a hoop. The grand finale was Tom pitting himself against Bruno in a wrestling match. The skirt was removed before the battle began.

At one performance Bruno was winning the match and Tom lost his temper. He tried to get a little rough with the bear and in response Bruno bit off one of Tom's fingers. But that did not end the tour. It did not even slow it down. Instead the boys capitalized on the unpleasant incident by advertised the pet bear as "Bruno the Man Eater" and for proof all Tom had to do was hold up his mangled hand.

THE STUDEBAKER

It used to be that Saturday was like a holiday. Folks who lived in rural areas would set that day aside to travel to town for supplies and shopping. If they were lucky the families were able to ride in the relative comfort of a Studebaker wagon.

The Studebaker Company made a functional all-purpose wagon. It was built strong and was extremely reliable. A Studebaker was easily recognized. The running gear was painted a bright red or yellow and the wagon box was always green with some scrollwork to fancy it up.

It was not uncommon for a farmer living in the East to be stricken by a case of wanderlust and decide to load all the family's belongings in the Studebaker, hitch up the team of faithful horses and head west over the Oregon Trail to the land of promise and free homestead land. When their destination was reached the Studebaker, when not used as a means of transportation, could be employed to carry a variety of rural necessities from water barrels to barbed wire, salt, grain, hay, and lumber.

In 1903 Henry Ford formed the Ford Motor Company and began mass-producing automobiles. Fifteen million Model-Ts were sold and the Studebaker wagon became a relic of the past. Farmers parked their wagons out behind the barn or at the edge of a field. In summer the sun bleached the wood and snow drifted over it in the winter. Years passed and the faithful old Studebaker wagon slowly crumbled and settled into the earth.

THE FISH

The fall of 1913 Orval Sannan and a group of friends from the small town of Promise hiked down to spend the day fishing, picnicking and relaxing along the Grande Ronde River.

Orval was the fisherman of the group but after several hours without a bite he announced, "I'm going to cross to the other side. Fishing's got to be better over there."

The others watched as Orval waded into the water. The stream was deep and the current comparatively slow. He called back over his shoulder, "I'm going to leave my line out. Maybe a big one will take my bait while I'm swimming across."

Orval reached a point where the water was waist deep and then, placing his fishing pole in his mouth to free his hands, he started swimming. His head was suddenly jerked under water. Twice he managed to fight his way to the surface and each time he was flailing his arms wildly. The other's thought he was trying to be funny. They laughed at his silly antics.

But the third time Orval went under he did not come up. His body was located fifty yards downstream from where he was last seen and a few feet away, also on the bottom, was the fishing pole. It was recovered and when the line was reeled in a 17-inch fish dangled from the hook.

The logical explanation for Orval's drowning was that the fish had hit the bait and dashed downstream. Since Orval had the fishing pole in his mouth this sudden action caused his head to dip below the surface and he must have inhaled a lethal dose of water into his lungs.

BLACKSMITH SHOP

The blacksmith shop was at the heart of every western community. On all but the coldest days of winter the big weathered doors stood wide open, inviting all who passed that way to stop. It was a wonderful place, full of unusual things to see and smell.

In the middle of the shop was the forge, a square red brick structure on an elevated platform. Hot flames danced in the forge and although a hooded chimney carried the smoke outside, it had a habit of finding its way back in through the open doors.

The blacksmith, shirtless and heavily muscled, stood at the forge, pumping a lever to operate the bellows which blew air into the fire, making it burn hotter. Long-handled tongs held the metal he was heating and when it was red-hot the smith carried it to the anvil and shaped it by beating it with a heavy hammer, reheating and hammering it over and over until he had the right shape. He tempered the metal by plunging it into a barrel of water and it hissed and gave off a cloud of vapor.

Often a horse stood in the shop impatiently pawing the ground as the smith fit shoes to its hooves. During the day, while the smith worked, drummers and other traveling men stopped to rent horses and buggies. After school the town children came to the blacksmith shop to see what was going on. They watched for a while and then hurried home to do their chores before supper.

Gray

THE HOLDUP

John McNamer grew up fast. As a boy he came west over the Oregon Trail and by the time he was 16 years old he was a volunteer soldier fighting in the Indian wars.

After the Indians were subdued John drifted south to California and caught on driving stagecoach on a Wells Fargo route between Redding and the mines.

On October 24, 1875 John was making a run, hauling a strongbox and three passengers. He was driving a six-horse team along a twisting mountain trail when an armed masked man suddenly stepped from behind a tree. He pointed a rifle at John and ordered, "This is a hold-up. Throw down the strongbox."

John reined the horses in and did exactly as he was instructed. He tossed the strongbox to the ground and said, "You've got the money. Can I clear out?"

"Get goin'," growled the robber.

John moved the horses ahead about a quarter mile and stopped. He set the brake, tied off the lines and climbed down. After whispering to the passengers, "Stay put and stay quiet," he started back.

There was the sharp crack of a rifle and John figured the robber had blown the lock on the strongbox. He continued forward, slipping from tree to tree until he had a commanding view of the masked man bent over the open Wells Fargo strongbox, counting the cash.

"Hold it right there!" John called out. "I've got the drop on you. Stand up nice and slow. Get your hands over your head."

For his heroic action Wells Fargo rewarded John with a gold pocket watch. But the local school fund was the real winner. The schools received the robber's pocket change — all $1,025.

TUSKO

Tusko was billed as the largest elephant in captivity. He stood a tremendous 12 feet 2 inches at the shoulders and weighed 7 solid tons.

Tusko was born in the wilds but was captured and trained to be a circus elephant. During his performances it appeared that Tusko was a docile giant but his trainers knew there was a dark side to the big animal. The wild had never left Tusko.

Once in Los Angeles Tusko attacked and killed a lion. Another time he had gone on a rampage overturning automobiles and even derailing a boxcar before he was recaptured. On Christmas Day 1931, Tusko was being held in a ramshackle shed at the foot of Southeast Main in Portland, Oregon. His legs were chained to four posts.

Two circus employees were assigned to watch over Tusko. They claimed that without provocation the elephant began trumpeting, shaking his massive head from side to side and tugging at the chains. He managed to break two of the chains, one on a front leg and one on a back leg. This allowed him room to move and he promptly knocked down a wall.

A local radio station sent a man to the scene and his reports drew a crowd of curious people. The elephant continued to struggle. He freed his other front foot and now, held only by one hind foot, he destroyed the shed from around him. The crowd cheered.

And then as quickly as the rage had swept over him it subsided and Tusko stood still, his sides heaving in and out from the exertion. Circus employees quickly placed hay and water in front of him and succeeded in refastening the chains. Never again was Tusko forced to perform in front of a circus crowd. He lived out his days in Woodland Park Zoo in Seattle.

BOYHOOD MEMORIES

Ed Snipes rubbed the silver stubble on his chin and recalled, "My older brother Ben left Iowa for the promised land. He wrote glowing accounts of the opportunities that existed out west and this caused Father to pack a prairie schooner and take to the trail. I was only six years old and rode a mule all the way.

"While we were on our way, Ben drove a herd of steers up to the Caribou mines on the Fraser River of Canada and sold them to the miners for one hundred dollars a head. He returned south, bought another herd and started all over again.

"When we landed in the Yakima Valley I went to work for Ben buckarooing and driving cattle. I remember the time we took 2,000 head of steers to Montana, drove them through the country and scarcely a house was seen on the way, only Indian tepees.

"Ben operated by buying cattle, grazing them on the public domain and selling them at a huge profit. He built up his herd to the point where he was running better than a hundred thousand head.

"A few bad winters set him back considerable but it was the financial panic of 1893 that finally did him in. Cattle prices fell so low you couldn't give away a cow. I had to quit buckarooing and find me a regular job."

TERRIBLE TRAGEDY

Jesse Applegate was seven years old when his family traveled the Oregon Trail. Upon reaching the Columbia River they built flat-bottomed boats and continued their journey by water.

According to Jesse's recollections a terrible tragedy occurred as they floated down the Columbia. "As we approached a bend in the river I could hear the sound of rapids… when looking across the river I saw a smaller boat about opposite us near the south bank.

"In this boat were three men and three boys, one being my brother and the other two cousins... it disappeared and we saw the men and boys struggling in the water. Father and Uncle Jesse, seeing their children drowning, were seized with frenzy, and dropping their oars, sprang up from their seats and were about to leap from the boat to make a desperate attempt to swim to them when Mother and Aunt Cynthia, in voices that were distinctly heard above the roar of the rushing waters, by commands and entreaties brought them to a realization of our own perilous situation, and the madness of an attempt to reach the other side of the river by swimming.

"They called out, 'Men, don't quit the oars. If you do we will all be lost.' The men returned to the oars just in time to avoid, by great exertion, a rock against which the current dashed with such fury that the foam and froth upon its apex was as white as milk. I sat on the right-hand side of the boat and the rock was so near I thought if we had not passed so quickly I might have put my hand on it."

RIDING THE STAGE

Stagecoach passengers were required to sit on uncomfortable wooden benches that faced each other. When the stage moved it creaked and swayed on its leather springs and the ride was punctuated by violent bumps and jolts that tended to throw the passengers together. In summer the dust boiled through the open windows and passengers tied bandanas across their faces so they could breath. In winter a lap blanket was necessary to help minimize the cold drafts.

The stagecoach driver sat outside on a high perch and used long lines to control the six or eight horses that comprised the team. Whatever dilemma was encountered it was up to the driver to figure a way out of the predicament. If a tree had blown over the road he had to find a way around the obstacle, or cut a way through. He might decide, on a whim, to take a muddy sinkhole at full gallop. And if the stage sunk to the hubs the driver had the authority to order the passengers out. Whether they were men in business suits or women in petticoats and long dresses, the passengers had no choice but to help push the stage out of the mud.

The driver might elect to wait at a flooded river crossing for the water to recede and the passengers knew better than to offer their opinion or advice. The rule of the road was that if a passenger had a suggestion to propose to the driver it was best to take it to the far side of the ridge before uttering it.

Until the stagecoach pulled into the station at the end of the journey the driver was king. And in the driver's estimation all the passengers were equal whether they owned a bank or only a bedroll.

BORN SHOWMEN

Bennie and Willie Goldstein were newspaper hawkers extraordinaire and born showmen to boot. They earned the most money of any newsboys in the city because they gave a performance with every newspaper they sold.

Bennie was a couple years older than his brother. He stood on the street corner shouting out the headlines while directing Willie to perform a variety of tricks to catch the attention of a potential customer. "Willie, do a handstand for this gentleman," or, "Willie, walk on your hands," or, "Willie, do a one arm push-up," or, "Willie, do the splits."

Willie was a talented acrobat and a gifted entertainer. He dressed in a well-worn, double-breasted jacket and mismatched slacks with holes in the knees. His routines always attracted a crowd but in spite of his efforts newspaper sales occasionally lagged. Whenever sales slowed the brothers resorted to some truly devious methods to sell their remaining newspapers.

Willie might sit on the curb, wailing loudly while tears streamed down his cheeks. Bennie would tell passersby a variety of believable stories. It might be, "Them other kids, they beat up poor Willie." Or he might claim he was only helping out the boy. "His father's sick and the family ain't got no food in the house."

If these ruses failed to sell the newspapers Bennie would shove a paper into the hands of a stranger and tell him, "Take it. If we go home and the papers ain't all gone Father he'll beat us with his razor strap." Usually the stranger paid the price of the paper.

One time a reporter interviewed the brothers and when questioned about their future plans Bennie responded, "All we want in life is to make a million bucks. That's it."

BUYING A BABY

Mrs. Himes was cooking over an open fire when a band of mounted Indians, wearing eagle feathers in their braided hair, fine buckskin shirts and britches decorated with colorful beads and porcupine quills, swept inside the protective circle of wagons.

Alarmed at the sight of Indians Mrs. Himes instinctively moved toward her one-year-old blue-eyed, golden-haired daughter sitting nearby on a blanket. The Indians stayed on their ponies and watched the child intently while Mr. Himes and the other men stood ready with their rifles. Several long minutes passed and then the Indians abruptly departed.

The following morning the Indians returned driving before them a large herd of ponies. They allowed the ponies to graze near the camp while they rode in. With a mixture of sign language and words one of the Indians let it be known he wanted to trade the ponies for the white girl with the golden hair.

Mrs. Himes was aghast. "No!"

The Indian stated that his own daughter had died of measles brought into the country by the white man. He explained it was Indian custom to purchase another baby. He wanted the white baby and offered more ponies.

"No! No! No! A thousand times no!" Mrs. Himes cried.

The Indian pounded a fist against his chest and lamented, "My heart sick." He spun his pony and galloped away.

WRECK OF THE *PETER IREDALE*

The skeletal remains of the ship *Peter Iredale* lie on a lonely stretch of sand near the mouth of the Columbia River.

Back in the fall of 1906 the grain-laden *Peter Iredale* departed from Salina Cruz, Mexico and sailed up the West Coast in light winds. A few miles shy of the mouth of the Columbia River the canvas came to life in a fresh breeze and the ship creaked and groaned under the strain of the billowing sails.

The sudden squall caught the crew off guard. They ran to man their stations as the wind blew sea spray off the top of the waves. The fury of the storm disoriented the crew and within a few minutes the *Peter Iredale* had run aground on the soft sand of the Clatsop Spit. The main masts snapped in two and the sails tumbled into the crashing surf.

In the nearby town of Hammond a rescue party was quickly organized and Captain Lawrence and his crew were rescued. As Captain Lawrence set foot on the beach he pulled a whiskey bottle from inside his coat, turned toward his floundering ship and toasted her with, "May God bless you and may your bones bleach in the sand." He saluted her, took a pull off the jug and passed it to his first mate. One by one the crew drank and said their good-bys to their faithful ship.

Today the *Peter Iredale* lies rusting on the beach. The metal hull is sunk deep in the sand and the ribs resemble a fish stripped to the bone. In time the relentless waves and the shifting sand will claim the last trace of the *Peter Iredale.*

LUCKY HANS

It was the last day of summer vacation. Hans Hansen and a friend were determined to make the most of it so they went on a fishing trip above the big falls on Cook Creek. Their theory was that the trout would be bunched up there.

The boys crawled through the thick undergrowth and were near enough that they could hear the distant roar of the falls. Hans was smaller and could move more quickly than his friend. He reached the creek and called back, "Perfect. I'm right here at the top of the falls."

Hans selected a straight willow and used his jackknife to cut it off. He tied line on the narrow end and was concentrating on skewering a fat worm on the hook when he had a strange sensation that he was being watched. Expecting to see his friend, he turned and was shocked to see a tawny-colored mountain lion. The cat snarled, hissed and showed its sharp teeth. Hans stood up, stepped back and caught his heel on an exposed root. He lost his balance and fell into the stream.

Hans flailed wildly with his arms and kicked with his feet as the swift current swept him downstream. At the very brink of the falls Hans was poised for an instant, and then the rushing water pushed him over the edge. As he plunged downward Hans never gave up trying to swim up the column of falling water. His effort proved futile and he was slammed into the boiling pool. Tons of white water pushed him down and an underwater volcano seemed to roar in his ears. He was almost out of air when he suddenly shot to the surface.

The next day at school, when the teacher asked the students what they had done on their vacations, Hans had a fantastic story to tell.

POOR BILLY

The Thomas family, including nine children, crossed the plains by wagon in 1851. At the summit of the Blue Mountains in Oregon they laid over a day at Emigrant Springs to rest the stock.

The men worked on the wagons, making necessary repairs and tightening the wheel rims in anticipation of the long descent to the rocky Columbia plateau. The women made bread as they waited for the big tubs of wash water to heat over the open fires. The children ran around yelling and playing a game of tag.

Nancy Thomas spread a quilt in the sunshine and laid her youngest child, one-year-old Billy, on it. She busied herself kneading dough, occasionally glancing from her work, as mothers will do, to check on little Billy. Her private thoughts were interrupted by a scream from one of the women. Nancy instinctively looked toward Billy and was terrified to see a mountain lion standing over the quilt. The cat opened its mouth, scooped up Billy and bounded away.

The men grabbed their rifles and gave chase. At the entrance to a cave the cat dropped Billy and turned to face its pursuers. The mountain lion, which proved to be a female with two kittens in the cave, was shot.

Billy was safe. Although his clothing had been torn, and there were teeth marks in his soft skin, he never even cried. In later years Bill Thomas became district judge of Wrangle, Alaska.

THE KID AND THE FOOTRACE

Back in the late 1860s a baby-faced, skinny kid roamed the West searching for unsuspecting runners to engage in footraces for money. His immature looks were deceiving. The kid actually was a trained circus performer and a professional foot racer.

To his credit the kid was a neat dresser, extremely polite and a talkative sort. His appearance in a town usually coincided with a county fair or some celebration that would guarantee a large crowd. His scheme was to strike up a cordial conversation with a group of men about some innocuous subject like the weather or fishing prospects and work the discussion around to the topic of foot racing.

"I'm pretty fast," he would brag, "anyway, pretty fast for a kid." In due time he would offer to run against the local champion, telling the men, "I've got some money. I'll take your bets."

One time the kid was put up against a burly farmer. The farmer agreed to a footrace on the condition he be allowed to name the place and distance.

"Fine by me," the kid said with a confident smile. After all bets were placed, the farmer led the way to the edge of town. He pointed to a freshly plowed field and announced, "We'll race to the far fence and back."

The kid got off to a fast start but soon tired in the soft soil. He had the speed but not the strength of the farmer and before long the kid was having trouble even lifting his feet. The farmer was the clear-cut winner.

That day the kid learned a valuable lesson — merely being fast on your feet does not always win the race. Sometimes you have to use your head, too.

THE TEACHER

A young man educated on the East Coast came west because he had read all of Zane Grey's books and wanted to experience the wide-open spaces and the challenge of becoming a school teacher on the frontier.

The prospective teacher took the train to a western city, caught a room at the hotel and busied himself applying for every opening in the field of education within a hundred-mile radius. One remote school district called him for an interview. It took twelve hours on the seat of a buckboard before he finally came to the small settlement with a one-room school.

That evening he met with the school board, five men who chewed tobacco, spit in gallon coffee cans and fidgeted with pocketknives. They looked at the young man skeptically and fired questions at him about his background and credentials. He took his time answering, thoroughly examining what he was going to say before he spoke and stringing his words together into thoughtful and concise sentences.

The five board members talked in quiet tones among themselves and then the chairman stated, "We have come to the conclusion you can have the job if you answer this final question the right way. Would you teach that the world is round or that the world is flat?"

The young man thought for a long moment. He was desperate for a job and did not know for sure how backwards the people were in this part of the country. At length he replied confidently, "Gentlemen, I am willing and prepared to teach it either way."

He was hired on the spot.

SHEEPHERDER

Around the turn of the 20th century young men from the Pyrenees mountains of Europe were brought to American to herd the great bands of sheep that roamed the West. These Basque herders were excellent sheep men with the ability to take a band onto the open range in the early summer and bring back fat, healthy animals in the fall. The bands of sheep, usually numbering between one and two thousand ewes and their lambs, grazed as they traveled. It was up to the herder and the herder's dogs to keep the sheep together and moving.

A herder directed his dogs with a combination of commands given by voice, whistles and hand signals. The best dogs constantly doubled back and around the band to keep the wanderers close and move the stragglers forward.

During the night the sheep would be gathered in the bottom of an open basin and the dogs were on constant patrol, driving away wild intruders. It was imperative for the Basque herders and their dogs to keep the sheep together because if a lamb or ewe ever became separated from the band it had a very short life expectancy. As darkness descended the separated animal was usually hunted down and killed by coyotes, cougars, bobcats or bears.

HERO

Michael Haney was a frail kid. He ran away from home when he was 17 years old to escape the teasing of his schoolmates and headed west. He hopped freight trains and when he ran low on money he stopped and worked a few days before moving on.

For a time he worked in the hop harvest. One payday Michael was walking along the riverbank when he heard a cry for help. He spotted a figure bobbing in the water and as the current swept the man near shore Michael reached out and tried to rescue him. But instead Michael was pulled into the water.

Michael and the drowning victim were swept into a rapid. They were turned and twisted in the churning white water and then, near the base of the swift current, they were pulled underwater in a swirling whirlpool for several long seconds before bobbing to the surface.

The drowning man, trying to save himself, grabbed hold of Michael. Michael, flailing his arms wildly, tried to swim for two and inch by inch he made his way toward shore. Some of the other hop pickers called encouragement. As Michael reached shallow water they waded in and helped him drag the victim to dry land where they pried the man's hands from around Michael's shoulders.

When the man who had come so close to drowning had recovered enough to speak he said his name was Harry Howard and he marveled at how such a spindly lad could have saved him. He shook Michael's hand and told him, "You're a hero."

KING OF THE COLUMBIA

Ranald McDonald was born in 1824 at the fur trading post of Fort Astoria. His mother was Princess Sunday, daughter of Comcomly, chief of the Chinook nation. His father was Archibald McDonald, a Scotsman in the service of the Hudson's Bay Company.

In 1831 an important event occurred that changed the course of Ranald's life. That year a Japanese vessel wrecked near Cape Flattery and three crewmen survived. Ranald met the men and vowed that one day he would visit Japan.

Shortly after Ranald turned 18 years old he signed aboard a whaling ship bound for the North Pacific. As the ship neared the coast of Japan Ranald purchased one of the ship's lifeboats and set off alone across the sea.

At that time Japan was closed to the outside world. When Ranald landed on Japanese soil he was promptly arrested. He claimed he had been shipwrecked but the Japanese had little sympathy for his plight. He eventually won over his captors and became the first to teach the English language to the Japanese.

For half a century Ranald lived a reclusive life until 1893 when he made a pilgrimage to Astoria and demanded title to all the land that was once held by the Chinook nation. The government ignored his claim and Ranald wandered up the Columbia River where he died among the tumbled-down ruins of abandoned Fort Colville.

THE TRIP WEST

Lucy Henderson was a young child when her family came west by wagon. She recalled, "On the way to Oregon my little sister Lettie passed away. Father made a coffin for her and we buried her there by the roadside in the desert.

"Three days after our terrible loss we stopped for a few hours and my sister Olivia was born. It was so late in the year that the men of the party decided we could not tarry even a day, so we had to press on. The going was terribly rough. The men walked beside the wagon and tried to ease the wheels down into the rough places, but in spite of this it was a very rough ride for my mother and her newborn babe.

"After eight months on the road we made it to Oregon. We were out of food and our cattle were nearly worn out. We had no choice but to leave our wagons in the mountains and with Mother on one horse holding her six-week-old baby in her lap, and with one of the little children sitting behind her, and with the rest of us riding behind the different men, we made it safely to the Willamette Valley.

"We lived on boiled wheat and boiled peas. So passed the first winter."

MAN OF THE FAMILY

"My father was a quiet man," recalled Willie Smith. "I remember the night he informed Mother and me that he was tired of fighting the drought in Iowa where he was trying to scratch a living from a dryland farm. He said we were going to make a fresh start of it out west.

"I was only seven years old at the time but I still remember he held his pearl-handled pocketknife and whittled while he talked. The knife blade flashed in the firelight while he promised that life would be better when we got settled in Oregon. I believed him.

"Come spring we joined a wagon train. At the end of each day the men would sit around the campfire and swap stories. But Father never joined in the revelry. Instead, he hiked off into the twilight to hunt for meat. He was an excellent marksman and he often returned after dark with a rabbit, a sage hen, sometimes even an antelope.

"One evening he failed to return. We were in Indian country and we tried to prepare ourselves for the worst. In the morning a group of men who had gone out in search of Father found his body. It appeared he had killed an animal, stooped over it and his pistol fell from his waistband and accidentally discharged when it hit the ground.

"The men brought Father's body back to camp. When they laid him on a pile of bedding his pearl-handled knife fell from his pocket. Mother scooped it up and handed it to me. She said, 'This is yours. Now you're the man of the family.'"

INDIAN HUMOR

The Bannock Indians went on the warpath in the summer of 1878. A group of daring men rode through the outlying countryside warning the settlers.

When the Carlile family heard the news they left their homestead on Willow Creek and fled into the mountains. When they figured the danger had passed they returned home expecting to find that the Indians had burned their cabin and barn to the ground.

But the buildings were still standing, though it was evident from the items scattered around that the Indians had been there and ransacked the place. Mr. Carlile cautiously approached the cabin. He pushed open the door and peered inside.

With a terrifying screech a four-footed, feathered creature burst from the dark interior, ran across the yard and leaped into a tree. Mrs. Carlile screamed but recovered quickly and demanded to know, "What was that?"

Mr. Carlile, his rifle ready, peered up into the tree. The creature meowed at him. It was the family cat.

The mystery of how the cat came to wear a coat of feathers was quickly solved. Apparently the Indians had dipped the cat in a keg of molasses and applied a liberal coating of feathers from a feather mattress.

The Carliles thought little of the practical joke. They coaxed the cat out of the tree and sheared it.

CHRISTMAS DINNER

It was the day before Christmas 1858 and the Himes family had nothing special to eat for Christmas dinner. Then a miracle fell from the sky.

Fourteen-year-old George was walking near the small lake behind the family's homestead cabin when a large flock of ducks circled low and landed on a pocket of open water on the frozen lake. George reasoned that if they could not have turkey for dinner then duck would certainly do. But George did not have his rifle with him and fearing the ducks would fly away if he went back after it, he desperately looked around for a weapon. All he saw was a round stone. He bent over and picked it up.

As soon as he exposed himself and threw the stone the flock moved in unison, beating the water white with their wings and leaping into startled flight. As they rose and flew away one lone duck remained, floating on the water. George yelled, "I got one! I got one!"

Then it hit him — how was he going to retrieve his prize? He could think of only one way. He grabbed a chunk of wood and beat it against the ice until it broke. And then, stepping gingerly into the cold water, he began to make his way toward the duck.

The following day, as the Himes family feasted on a Christmas dinner of roasted duck, George knew that his efforts had been worth it.

GRAIN HARVEST

Grain harvest was an exciting time of the year, ranking right up there with the 4th of July and Christmas. There was plenty to see and to do during harvest as neighbors worked together, sharing horses and mules, machinery and manpower.

Binders, pulled by horses or mules, cut and bound the wheat, dropping it in the field for men to pick up and load onto wagons and transport to the thresher. The stationary steam-powered thresher was the center of the operation. It chewed through sheaves of wheat, separating the grain and blowing away the straw and chaff. The grain was sacked, loaded on horse-drawn wagons and taken to storage.

The men and older boys worked in the fields, the women cooked and the youngsters helped carry the platters of food to a series of tables and wooden planks set on sawhorses. There was fried chicken and smoked hams, mashed potatoes, stacks of steaming corn on the cob, fresh-churned butter, hot biscuits, corn bread, jam, jelly, gallons of milk, and cake and cookies for dessert.

After eating, and taking a few minutes to allow the hearty meal to settle, the men returned to the fields while the women and children cleared the tables and began washing the small mountain of dishes.

STRANGE CAT

John Corbett and his wife operated Rattlesnake Stage Station. They employed a young Chinese boy to wash dishes and help prepare meals. The boy was a hard worker but he had one peculiarity — he was obsessed with kittens and cats.

But trying to keep a cat at the stage station was a challenge. Each time one of the stage drivers brought the boy a cat it disappeared and then he moped around and did very little work. John told the boy, "I know what's happening to the cats. Rattlesnakes are killing them. So forget about trying to keep a cat around the place. No more cats. Do you understand?"

The boy nodded that he understood but he begged for just one more cat or kitten, promising he would keep it indoors. John steadfastly refused, repeating, "No more cats."

One afternoon the Chinese boy called to Mrs. Corbett to come see the pretty kitty. She stepped into the kitchen and was mortified to catch sight of the boy reaching behind the stove to pet a ball of black and white fur. She spoke sharply, "That's a skunk! Stay away!"

Her warning came too late. The skunk sprayed the boy and the foul odor permeated the kitchen. When the evening stage arrived the driver and passengers took one whiff and decided they were not very hungry after all.

ROVING SPIRIT

Sixteen-year-old Maria Smith had a roving spirit. She claimed what she wanted most from life was to become a world traveler and see new places.

One evening at supper her father announced the family was moving to Oregon. Maria whooped with joy and flew out the door to tell her friends. She would not have been so happy if she had known all the hardships that awaited the family on the Oregon Trail crossing.

First they encountered hostile Indians along the Platte River. An arrow fired from a willow thicket narrowly missed Maria, sailing past her and killing one of the oxen. Then, shortly after crossing the Continental Divide at South Pass, the leaders of the wagon train took a shortcut. The trail they followed led through dry, desolate country with very little feed for the stock and hardly any water. The wagons had to be abandoned and the remaining supplies were packed on the backs of the oxen while the emigrants were forced to walk.

Although none of the emigrants died they suffered terribly before eventually reaching the Willamette Valley, arriving just before Christmas 1846. Mr. Smith took a donation land claim on rich bottom ground bordering the Luckamute River.

When Maria reached legal age she took an adjoining land claim. Apparently her adventuresome spirit and desire to travel had been satisfied because for the remainder of her life she was content to live on her homestead along the Luckamute River.

FAMOUS BERT

When the Maris family took in the orphan boy they never could have imagined that some day little Bert would become the most powerful man in the world.

"When Bert first came to us my wife told him she cut the other boys' hair and she might just as well cut his hair, too," recalled N.C. Maris. "He told her to go ahead. After she finished, he asked, 'Ma'am, how much do I owe?'

"Mother, she can be something of a tease. She looked him up and down and pronounced, 'Well, I did a mighty fine job. I guess a quarter would be about right.'

"A look of anguish swept over Bert's face and slowly, very slowly, he reached in his trouser pocket and produced a single quarter, all the money he had in the world, and handed it to her. She laughed, told him it was a joke and to keep his money.

"But that was Bert, he was a real serious kid. He did his chores faithfully; milked the cow, fed the pigs, mucked manure out of the stalls, brought in the wood. After his work was done he would stick his nose in a book. He was a bookworm and read good books."

In school Bert was an excellent student. After graduating from high school he enrolled at Stanford University and earned a degree in mining engineering. He traveled the world managing various mining operations and became a millionaire several times over. In 1929 Bert, better known as Herbert C. Hoover, was sworn in as the 31st President of the United States.

LONG WAY HOME

Billy Jackson was just a boy of 18 when he left home and enlisted in the Confederate Army.

In his first battle he was captured and sent north on a transport train to the Union prison at Alton, Illinois. Along the way he managed to unbolt a window cover, jump from the moving train and escape.

Billy kept to the back roads, traveling only at night. His destination was his home in Missouri. As he walked he thought of his mother and father and of his brothers and sisters. Those memories sustained him.

Early one morning he was surprised by a booming voice, "What's your company?" Billy froze. A second later he felt the barrel of a rifle shoved into his ribs.

"You won't shoot me like a dog," Billy told the Union soldier as he pushed away the rifle muzzle and broke into a run. But a force slammed into his shoulder with the weight of a swung anvil, followed by a thundering boom. Billy fell but jumped up and continued to run.

After being wounded Billy traveled fewer miles each day. He endured the pain in his shoulder and finally he reached home only to find his family gone. According to Nanny, a slave who had stayed on, Billy's parents had tired of the war and left by wagon train for Oregon.

Billy stayed in Missouri until his wound healed and then he, too, started west. He arrived in Salem the fall of 1865 and was reunited with his family.

JUST PLAYING

The Kranick family lived on a remote homestead. The children, Les, Gladys and Nellie, walked to and from school on a narrow, twisting trail through the deep woods. They always stopped halfway to rest.

Here a small creek tumbled in a showy waterfall off a basalt cliff. The ground water was close to the surface and the trail was always boggy. Most days Les fiddled with a stick, digging a series of channels to help drain the water, while his sisters nibbled on a treat from their lunch baskets.

One morning Les had the bright idea to kill time by making animal tracks in the soft mud. He had seen mountain lion tracks and knew how to make them using his knuckles. The tracks he made certainly looked authentic. To add a little drama he encouraged Gladys and Nellie to walk along the trail and he followed behind them making mountain lion tracks in their footprints.

Later that day a passerby noticed the tracks and when he reached town he spread the word a mountain lion was stalking children on the trail up the river canyon. His story was even printed in the evening newspaper.

The following day at school Les heard about the excitement he had caused. There was talk of organizing a hunting expedition and bringing in bloodhounds. Les figured it was only a matter of time before the hounds tracked him to school. He confessed to his teacher, telling her he just had been playing mountain lion.

ORPHANS OF THE TRAIL

Henry Sager was a restless man. He moved his family from Ohio to Missouri and then decided to continue westward over the Oregon Trail.

His young daughter Catherine later wrote of that terrible experience: "We started off and on the 22nd of May Mother surprised us by the arrival of another little sister. That made 7 of us children.

"One day I went to jump from the wagon without putting Father to the trouble of stopping the team. In performing this feat, the hem of my dress caught on an axle-handle, precipitating me under the wheel which passed over me, badly crushing the left leg.

"And then outside Fort Laramie Father was trapped in a buffalo stampede and seriously injured. It soon became apparent to all that he would die. As I lay helplessly by his side, he said, 'Poor child! What will become of you?'

"After we buried Father the nights and mornings were bitter cold. Mother was afflicted with the sore mouth that was the forerunner of the fatal fever. She soon became delirious."

When Mrs. Sager died she was buried beside the trail. The seven Sager children, ranging in age from fourteen to the youngest, only a few weeks old, were left orphans. The children continued to travel with the wagon train until they reached the missionary settlement of Marcus and Narcissa Whitman. The Whitmans, who had recently lost a baby, adopted and cared for the Sager children.

Gray

Rick Steber's Tales of the Wild West series feature illustrations by Don Gray. The AudioBooks are narrated by Dallas McKennon. Current titles in the series include:

OREGON TRAIL Vol. 1 *
PACIFIC COAST Vol. 2 *
INDIANS Vol. 3 *
COWBOYS Vol. 4 *
WOMEN OF THE WEST Vol. 5 *
CHILDREN'S STORIES Vol. 6 *
LOGGERS Vol. 7 *
MOUNTAIN MEN Vol. 8 *
MINERS Vol. 9 *
GRANDPA'S STORIES Vol. 10
PIONEERS Vol. 11
CAMPFIRE STORIES Vol. 12
TALL TALES Vol. 13
GUNFIGHTERS Vol. 14
GRANDMA'S STORIES Vol. 15
WESTERN HEROES Vol. 16
**Available on AudioBook CD*

Other books written by Rick Steber—

FORTY CANDLES
SECRETS OF THE BULL
BUY THE CHIEF A CADILLAC
BUCKAROO HEART
NEW YORK TO NOME
WILD HORSE RIDER
NO END IN SIGHT
HEARTWOOD
ROUNDUP
LAST OF THE PIONEERS
TRACES
RENDEZVOUS

www.ricksteber.com

Bonanza Publishing
Box 204
Prineville, Oregon 97754